Sea Men

Emmy looked at the dark water and bit her lip. Anything could be under there staring up at her and she would never know it. "I am not really a strong swimmer."

Bob grinned from next to her. "Don't worry. I am here to help."

She was about to ask him if she could skip the night swim when he used his larger muscle mass to grab her and pull her over the side and into the water.

She shrieked and choked on the water as she fought to right herself and tread on the surface. "Why did you do that?"

He chuckled and swam closer, his years of competitive swimming showing in the ease of his movements.

"You needed to get wet, and this was the fastest way to do it." The shadow of his face showed the white Cheshire-like grin.

She tried to move away from him. "I just don't appreciate death being an option."

He slipped over to block her from returning to the boat. "You can hold onto me if you like." He stroked his hand up her arm, and then, he cupped her breast.

She jerked back. "I told you; I am not interested."

He lunged forward and kissed her, holding her hair as they sank under the waves.

He held her there until she was weakly struggling before he kicked them back to the surface. He was grinning again. "If you say you'll fuck me, I will take you back to the boat."

She groaned at her stupidity. She had

Sea Men—A woman abandoned to the ocean for refusing to cross the friend-zone barrier finds herself the object of interest for some mermen as she loses her grip on reality.

Swipe Right—On a first date, her realtor companion decides to show her an un-sellable house. When he makes a move, she rebuffs him but not in time to stop his girlfriend from seeing them.

Cross Country—She is with friends and a guide on a skiing weekend, but she isn't as fast as her companions. After a flurry, she is lost and they are gone. Finding shelter is her prime concern with night creeping in, but the mythical beast she has to share a cave with has more than sleep on his mind.

Camping Out—After a stressful wedding, she is tired of being the bridesmaid. Now, here she is, forced to camp with friends while she remains in the only so-lo tent. She pitches her small site away

from the others. The scratch on her flap
in the middle of the night is definitely
something that wants to know her better
as it hauls her into the woods.

The characters and events in this book are fictitious. Any similarity to real persons, living or dead, is coincidental and not intended by the author.

The scenarios contain dubious consent and are not for all readers. It is erotic horror and should not be construed as anything else.

Published by Viola Masters

Dark Tales 1

By

Viola Masters

been told that everyone needed to try a midnight swim on their first time out on the ocean. All of her friends had agreed with long winks in Bob's direction. She had just wanted to fit in with the more affluent crowd. College sucked.

She frowned but stood her ground, so to speak. "No. I am not going to fuck you, but I am going back to the boat."

She started to swim toward it, and he simply swam around her, making it to the boat when she was still yards away. The engine fired up, and he looked at her over his shoulder. "Bitch."

He gunned the engine, and the small zodiac skimmed over the waves, leaving her alone in the dark.

She wanted to yell, but she had to keep her mouth shut. The choppy waves of the wake were trying to drown her.

Emmy aimed for the direction she remembered them being in and followed the wake of the boat to try and get to safety. She wasn't going to make it. She knew she was done for, but she wasn't giving up.

Her arms grew heavy, and it wasn't until something touched her leg under the water that a surge of adrenalin ripped through her. She couldn't shriek. She needed her mouth to breathe.

Another slick touch on her thigh made her keep going. She was terrified, but continuing toward her only hope of safety was her one chance. When a grasp around her ankle pulled her under, her mouth and nose flooded with salt water.

She tried not to breathe in, she saw bubbles coursing up to the light of the moon, and there was no way of knowing what had a grip on her. The water got darker and darker.

Her lungs were about to pop when a glowing figure appeared in front of her. It was vaguely masculine, and it held something in its grasp.

Cool metal clasped her neck and splayed over her chest between her breasts. Energy rippled along her skin and zipped through her bloodstream as her vision went black.

She didn't want to breathe in... didn't want to die. When she couldn't stand it, the blurry figure in front of her gripped her arms and shook her. Her burning lungs gave in and released the last of the air. She felt the water rush in.

The pressure on her skin burned where the cuff fastened her to the carved stone. She was floating above it, but the one shackle held her down to the ocean floor.

Glowing lichen lit up small pieces of the empty valley she was in, and the necklace that she could only see part of was glowing as well.

A shadow closed in on her, and a merman was examining her in detail. He touched her hair, her cheek and went down to her one-piece.

She looked at the man, took in the silver of his tail and noted the shape and direction of the fin at the end. He had a cloud of midnight hair, midnight eyes and wide gill slits running down his neck.

She flinched when he pulled on the strap of her suit, and he grinned, pulling her toward him in the water. He opened his mouth, and the wide, deadly expanse of teeth split his head nearly in two.

He bit through the fabric easily and did the same to the other strap.

She tried to touch his head, but he snapped at her as he peeled the spandex from her body, biting it free as necessary.

When the heavier elastic between her thighs fought his tugging, he swam down, pulled the fabric free of her and snapped quickly.

She nearly peed herself. Those teeth were so close to her groin that the brush of the deadly implements abraded her skin.

The fabric floated free of her body, and she tried to tug free of the cuff on her ankle. She hadn't felt it snap on.

The shark man floated in front of her, and his smile was cruel. His webbed hands gripped her breasts, and he pulled roughly at them, his skin abrading her nipples.

She shivered.

He pressed his lips to her breasts, scraping delicately against her skin with his teeth. She kept completely still.

She was either in hell or hallucinating. He kneaded at her flesh, and she could see something forming below his belly. The smooth skin was opening, and two large erections were swelling to an alarming size and shape.

This had to be a dream. Mermen

weren't real. Bob had abandoned her, and this was her mind's way of protecting her from the deadly reality as she drowned. That was it.

Perhaps if she let go, her departure from the world would be peaceful.

He pushed her to the edge of her tether and faced her as he gripped her hips. She reached between them and caressed the cocks that wobbled there. They were coated in a thick, slick coating, which was probably good, as her own lubrication wouldn't have a chance at letting him in.

His eyes were heavy lidded, and he stroked his fingers between her thighs before lining up one of his members. Her body clutched it tightly as it worked in.

To her embarrassment, he lined the other cock head with her ass, and he began to nudge it inside. He wasn't fully erect, and she knew it the moment he

was in both of her orifices and he continued to swell and harden.

She would have groaned, but the liquid in her lungs didn't allow for sound.
It was a silent fucking that began as he
moved in and out of her in a slow and
deep motion. The slick coating on his
cocks let him ease in and out with luxu-
rious thoroughness.

She clutched at his shoulders, and he
gnashed his teeth. She kept well away
from his deadly jaws as she was filled
beyond what she thought she could take.
He fucked her for what felt like hours
before she screamed and he shuddered
as if waiting for her signal.

He pressed his cheek to hers before
pulling out, leaving her sore, aching and
energized.

He swam away, and she was left staring into the dark waters and wondering
what was going to happen next. He
hadn't released her, so that meant she

wasn't done.

Shadows slid just beyond the glow of the light. Emmy bent down, grabbed the chain and pulled herself to the stone, looking for a way to unlock her confinement. It might be a dream, but she still wanted out of it.

A hand stroked her butt, and she turned to see a golden man behind her. Well, he was half man, the rest was brilliantly coloured with a wide fantail.

She was about to let go of the chain, but he wrapped his hands around hers and showed her what he wanted.

She wasn't facing him, so she guessed at what was about to happen. He was fully erect when he shoved his way into her ass, and she gasped for air that wasn't there. One of the shadows came toward her, and another merman of the traditional variety was in front of her, holding his cock.

He pushed it into her open mouth until the small, sharp scales around his pelvis pressed against her nose. She gagged, but whatever the coating on his cock was numbed her throat, and he began to thrust as his buddy pulled in and out of her ass with a heavy beat.

She was pinned and clutching the chain as they pistoned back and forth. Her body was the only anchor point for all three of them.

Her fingers got numb around the chain, as her grip became her focus. Her ass felt tight, and a dark pleasure was filling her.

The cock in her throat jerked, and the man floated away, strands of cum connecting them as his orgasm continued.

The merman behind her pounded faster until he shook and gripped her hips with his hands, digging his nails into her skin.

Her ass throbbed when he pulled out. She had been feeling a bit of arousal from the friction, but now, she was stuck and scanning the phantom world around her for another playmate.

Darkness flickered, and another merman came out. He was solid charcoal grey with a light in the centre of his forehead.

He took her hands off the chain and ran his hands up her arms. She bobbed toward him. He held her against him, and to her surprise, he kissed her.

He pressed her hands to his chest, and he held her, caressing her slowly, as if they were first-time lovers. He wove his hand through her hair and held her carefully, as if she was treasured.

She felt the smooth texture of his skin and ran her hands down his chest and around to his back. The thick ridge of spikes made her draw back.

He kissed her softly, licking at the inside of her mouth with a strangely pointed tongue. She licked back and felt his lips flex against hers. When their kiss escalated to the point where she would have been panting and moaning, he slid a hand between them and caressed the swollen lips between her thighs. In a fast beat, he pulled away from her mouth and moved down between her thighs. He draped one leg over his shoulder and the other was held in one of his hands. He pushed the pointed tongue into her, and she twisted, seeking an anchor for her flailing hands.

Another pair of hands helped her and held her while she rocked in the current to the rhythm of the tongue plunging into her.

Her vision spun, and she looked around for something, anything, to use to focus herself. Her first male, the shark, was there, holding onto her and holding her hands as the anglerfish had his way with her.

She moved with the beat as the pointed tongue worked higher and higher into her. Her body was nearly to the edge, she felt a quiver inside her, and just as she was about to go over, he pulled away.

To her shock, he pulled away from her and blew her a kiss. The shark released her, and she was floating alone again.

It felt like hours, but it could have been days, before the next shadow moved into the light.

Hard silver scales marked his tail. The fins were blades that appeared to be deadly. His body was a pale silver, and his eyes were the same absolute black as the others.

He had strange, wide lips, and his gaze was fixed on her. His thick tail undulated side to side as he approached. Her stomach flipped when he slid his hands up her ribs and cupped her breasts.

She moved her hands down his body, but he was too long. She couldn't touch his cock.

His tail wrapped around her and pulled her toward him until her ankle felt the pressure of the restraint. She wrapped one leg around him, and the smile that spread across his features was chilling.

She felt something *wiggling* against her, and her vantage point wouldn't let her see it. She stared into his eyes as the head of his cock wiggled into position in her sex. With a tightening of his tail, he pulled her forward while he thrust into her.

Emmy clutched at him, pushing and pulling him in turn as he went deep into her.

The water rushed in her ears, but she could feel the suction of her body pulling as he slid deeper with every thrust. When he was fully inside her, she was amazed that she could take him all.

As he started to twist and churn his cock inside her, she screamed silently as the unfamiliar sensation was confused for pain, pleasure and she didn't know what.

He continued to move inside her with a rapid corkscrew movement until he crushed her to him and his cock jerked within her.

Emmy floated back as he left her. Her body was screaming with aches and pains. Wasn't the afterlife supposed to be peaceful?

She might have slept, but when she felt a change in the very current around her, she angled upward and looked toward the flicker in the shadows. She was hanging upside down, so it took some manoeuvering to get her upright.

At first, she couldn't find the figure in the shadows until the tentacle moved forward, pulling the rest of the creature with it.

How a man could be fused with an octopus had never entered her mind. Mermen had a long history, so any of them could have been mixed with any species of fish. This was something entirely different.

The crown on the head of the man indicated that he was some kind of ruler. His approach was slow and deliberate.

His body was a rich purple. His tentacles were a few shades darker. The slow cascade of his limbs pulled him ever closer.

Was this purgatory? Did she need to spend time servicing these creatures before she passed on to her true reward, or was this punishment for deeds she didn't remember?

He continued to move slowly toward her until he was right in front of her. With a slight surge of his tentacles, he moved up to meet her, wrapping two of his limbs around her legs for support.

She looked into his eyes, and the dark orbs crinkled at the corners in a smile. He kissed her, and she welcomed him as his tongue thrust between her lips.

She didn't need to hold onto him; his tentacles held her arms behind her body, parted her legs and invaded her in one smooth movement.

He continued kissing her as the suction cups on his limbs attached to her to hold her fast and slowly twisted into her pussy with deliberate attention to the increasing girth of the tentacle.

She groaned silently as he filled her and another tentacle shifted into her ass. The small suction cup on her clit got her attention as it began to squeeze while the tip of the tentacle inside her writhed.

She fought against the pull of his limbs, but they wrapped tighter around her, holding her as he thrust into her with deliberate care.

Her orgasm hit her in a wave, and her body pulled and jerked against his grip. She tried to squirm away, but he continued to tease her, and another wave of heat started to run through her bloodstream.

She was stretched nearly to breaking, but whatever coated the mermen's cocks made it easy for the monster inside her to slide around.

Her arousal was slow to get to a critical level, but when she was clenching around him in desperation, he removed his tentacle and slid into her with a cock thicker than her wrist.

She fought the impalement as he moved into her, but he stroked her clit with an eager suction cup, and the squeezing and rubbing took her higher and eased his invasion.

His kisses were insistent that she pay attention, so she focused on him and met his eager lips with her own.

His cock took up all the space inside her, but the tentacle still in her ass massaged it via the thin membranes between them. She groaned and fought the grip that he held her in.

He slowly started to thrust, and on the fourth deep, aching slide into her, she bucked as she came. She would have screamed, but she couldn't.

She saw stars, but he continued to thrust over and over, holding her in an implacable grip.

Her body clenched around his twice more before he shuddered against her. He pulled out of her, and a dark ink trailed away from the thick stump of his cock.

Emmy was beyond exhausted, and she was about to relax when her lover turned back to her and wrapped a tentacle around her nose and mouth. Whatever she had been breathing was cut off and everything went dark.

"She's breathing, man! Get an ambulance. What the hell is that all over her?"

Emmy heard the roar around her, felt the sand under her abraded body, and she coughed up more water. *Holy shit. I am alive!*

The hospital treated her for the abrasions to her body, and they asked her her name. The moment the words were out of her mouth, she was silenced and the police were called.

The officer sat next to her and asked her, "What happened? Be as precise as you can, miss."

She blushed a little, but stuck to the pertinent information. "I was trying to swim back to the zodiac, but Bob took off and left me to teach me a lesson. I tried to follow his wake, but it was so dark. That is all I remember until the beach."

He nodded and got the particulars for her party.

"Why were folks so surprised by my name?"

"Oh, you have been missing for two years."

Emmy sat up straight. "That isn't possible."

Her nether region flexed in protest to her shift in position.

"It is. Your companions were suspects in your disappearance, but as there was no proof, they were never charged. They can at least be levied with depraved indifference for this action."

She smiled weakly and laid back. "Good. I am guessing that I have lost my apartment."

The officer smiled and leaned forward, patting her hand. "It will be taken care of. Victim's services handle this sort of thing."

Emmy nodded briefly, but she muttered, "But I was just there."

"Just where, miss?"

"I was chained by my ankle to the bottom of the sea, and mermen took turns with me. I thought it was just hours or days."

"Mermen? Have the doctors assessed you?"

She looked at him, and as she stared, his eyes flared black. She screamed and jolted back in the bed, getting as far away from him as she could.

He reached for her, and she shouted, slapping at his hands and trying to keep him away from her.

Nurses rushed in, and she was sedated. They held her down, and she kept eye contact with the dark-eyed officer until the drugs pulled her under.

Six weeks later, she was at the Seaside Gardens Rehabilitation Facility. Emmy went to therapy every day in an effort to purge her mind of the memories.

She wore loose clothing without a bra and was sitting in the gardens when one of the attendants came by to see her.

"Emmy? How are you today?" He sat next to her on the bench.

"Not bad. I finished a counselling session and now have the rest of the day to pretend I am normal. How are you, Davis?"

He grinned. "Pretty good."

They sat in silence for a moment before he asked her. "Have you had your period since you arrived?"

She shook her head. "No. The doc said I was stressed."

"They didn't do a rape kit?"

"I was apparently in the water for days. There was no point."

"Could you be pregnant?"

She paused, a chill running through her. "Not if I am sane. If I am sane, it is impossible. If I am insane, it could be."

She pressed a hand to her abdomen as if she could feel something.

"I am surprised they didn't do a blood test."

Emmy snorted, lost in the thought of motherhood. "They were worried about my being mauled by sea creatures. I had bites and marks from at least five different species. It must have happened when I got away from wherever I was."

"You don't look too upset." Davis smiled slightly.

"I am not. It isn't the ideal outcome, and if it was fathered during my time away, I am definitely going to have to go for a water birth in a tidal pool."

"You won't destroy it?"

"Well, it is either a figment of my imagination or a baby. Either way, destroying it won't change the fact that I can't take care of myself in the outside world."

A charity had offered to sponsor her

time at the facility, and she had jumped at the chance. If she was truly insane after her experiences, this was the safest place for her.

She leaned over and rubbed her ankle. She could still feel the cuff.

"Well, I just wanted to say hi. Have a good day, Emmy." He stood and paused, but she didn't look up.

"Good day, Davis."

She was lost in thought. A pregnancy could be possible if the human half of the monsters were true to species. They fucked like humans, so it was possible that they bred like them.

When it was time for lunch, she drifted in, looking for Davis to apologize for her distraction, but he was nowhere to be found.

Another six weeks went by, and she felt a swelling in her abdomen. Her clothing hid the bulge, so she didn't mention anything. It wouldn't do for the doctors to think she had seduced one of the staff to bring a kernel of possibility to her story.

She behaved herself and played sane when it came to therapy, finally earning herself a clean bill of mental health. She was going home the following week.

Late at night, in the quiet of her room, she heard the scuff of a foot near her door, and she opened her eyes. This was definitely unusual.

She could swear it was Davis walking toward her, but when she sat up to look, she saw black eyes and didn't even notice the needle that sedated her.

She opened her eyes a little while he carried her through the halls and out of the facility. The wind caressed her cheek as he walked toward the sea.

She thought he would just walk in, but they boarded a boat, and the engine hummed to life before droning as he took her far out to sea.

This was it. She was going to die. She had to shake this run of luck. She hated the thought of being in that cold water alone again.

"Oh. You are awake."

She flicked her eyes toward him as he calmly steered them out toward the rising sun.

"Apologies for the sedative. It couldn't be helped." He chuckled. "Did you know that out of three hundred women, you are the first to not only survive our attentions, but also carry a child from our bloodlines?"

She frowned. "It isn't true. They told me it couldn't be true."

The last three months of explanation and derision coursed through her mind.

"They haven't met us. We have hidden from the world and have been very successful at it." He kicked off his shoes.

His webbed toes looked familiar.

"How long was I down there?"

He shrugged. "It was a few years of surface time. We just couldn't stop playing with you. You are amazingly strong."

She shuddered as her body warmed at the idea of their *play*. "Why don't I remember the passage of time?"

He grinned, showing shark-like teeth. "We kept you very busy."

She looked out at the empty expanse of the sea and whispered, "Why didn't I die?"

"The box next to your hip. Put it on once we stop. It will allow you to breathe and suspend your aging."

She moved slowly, sluggishly. The box was carved stone with a trident on it. She opened it up, and her heart thudded in her chest. She knew that chain. It was the necklace that had been wrapped around her as she drowned.

"This kept me alive?"

"It did, like others before you. They weren't strong enough for us."

"Who is *us*?"

He smiled again. "Sons of Poseidon. We have been looking for mates for centuries, but it is hard to find women at our location. Let alone any that can accommodate all of us."

She shivered at that thought. "Is that all of you?"

"It is all that won the right to fuck you. The rest need to earn it."

She placed a hand over her belly. "What about the baby? If I am not aging, I will be pregnant indefinitely."

He grinned. "We have an island for that. Once you have the child, its father will take it and you will be free to mate with again."

"So, I won't get pregnant again with the necklace on."

He scowled. "No. We will have to work something out so that you have a chance to breed every few decades."

She looked around and tried not to look petrified. "How did you find me?"

"Arturad was the officer who spoke to you in the hospital. He is one of ours. He was surprised that you noticed his lack of control over his eyes. Few folks would have noticed."

She blinked at the weird compliment. "I was a little sensitive to the distinctive indicator."

There was nothing to see but the waves in any direction.

"Will the baby be hurt if I go under?"

He shook his head. "No. It will be fine. I will take you to the dry site that we have prepared for you. There is food and fresh water. Everything that you need."

"How long have you worked at the facility?"

"We keep an eye on our women after we leave them. Madness is a common side effect, but even there, you managed to keep your knowledge of the events in a fairly cogent version. Well done."

He was patting her on the head, and she knew it. With just her nightgown on, she could feel the cool breeze and the morning sunlight on her bare legs.

They continued for another few hours, and then, he cut the engine. The boat was simply bobbing in the middle of nowhere, and Davis stripped off his shirt before undoing his pants and unzipping them.

"Oh damn. I thought I imagined that."

"You handled them very well. I would enjoy it if you wanted to get used to them in this shape." He raised his eyebrows.

"I am not getting out of here."

"No. The gods sent you to us, and we will keep you."

There was no escape. She was going to be a sex toy for men out of her weirdest fantasies. May as well start now.

She knelt in front of him, examining the twin cocks that sprang side by side. She touched them and watched them swell.

She caressed the left and then the right before she wrapped her mouth around them in turn.

The abrasive texture of his other skin was not shared with his members. They were long, slick and throbbed in her hand as she sucked at the salty tips. The boat bobbed as she lapped at him, letting one of the cocks slip free and leave a slick trail on her cheek.

His voice was low. "Into the water. Now."

She looked up, and his human features were being stamped with the shark's.

She looked at the box and removed the necklace, taking it out and holding it in her clenched fist.

Davis casually lifted the box and held it over the edge before he dropped it in the water.

He smiled. "No clues."

She didn't know what he meant until he lifted her carefully and eased her over the edge and into the water. He revved the engine and jumped out as the boat took off.

Emmy took a deep breath and put the necklace on, feeling a solid click as she managed the latch.

Davis grinned, showing his sharp teeth, and he sank beneath the waves, grabbing her ankle and pulling her down.

She fought hard to hold her breath, but he shook her body and the air escaped. When she pulled in water at long last, he grinned at her, wrapped his arms around her and carried her down beyond the light.

She touched the swell of her belly beneath the sleeping gown and hoped that her body could stand the increasing pressure.

Shadowy figures joined their travels as Davis took her through cities of coral, pools of glowing light that popped up out of nowhere, and when the water grew absolutely black, the anglerfish shifter appeared to take over the lead.

Davis held her close, and their group moved as one in the darkest portion of the ocean. A change in the energy of the group indicated that they were close to wherever they were going.

Emmy relaxed and let them carry her through the sea, not convinced that this wasn't a hallucination that was going on for a ridiculously long degree.

She had snapped, and her mind had locked her in this dream. She had no way of knowing how to get free or if the way out was in giving in.

The bodies around her came in close

as they entered a cavern, lit by the anglerfish ahead of them. She felt limbs against hers, but the shadows around her were absolute. Davis's rough skin gave him away, but it could have been anyone next to her.

Their progress slowed until they could only move through one at a time, and the light that streamed from above made Emmy smile.

She reached up, and to her stunned surprise, her hand broke the surface of the water.

She still had water in her lungs and tried to speak, but nothing came out but gurgles. Davis lifted her head above the water and propelled her to the stone bank.

He shifted, stood and held her with her head down, draining her lungs before he removed the necklace.

The moment the necklace was off, she began to cough and throw up water.

The men were leaving the water, one at a time, taking on legs where fins had been. The octopus was the first to approach her, and he smiled. "Welcome to your new home, Emmy."

Davis made the introductions. "Emmy, this is Triton. Eldest son of Poseidon."

She didn't know how to greet him. Wasn't sure whether to bow or curtsey in her sodden nightgown.

He took the difficulty out of her hands by lifting her up and kissing her, threading his hand through her wet hair and holding her as he tasted her deeply.

His tongue thrust into her mouth and coaxed her into playing with him. When she was leaning up and pressing against him, he pulled back and released her, passing her to the next man over.

Again, Davis made the introductions before she was kissed senseless. Coreon was the anglerfish. His sharp tongue remained in his human form, and he ran his hands over her back, cupping her ass to pull her against him.

She shivered and held onto him until she was pried away and Leson then Arguon and Weson took her mouth.

When they had all greeted her, Triton looked at her belly. "Is it true?"

Davis grinned, and he moved between them to grip the neckline of her sleeping gown. He tore it in half and discarded the pieces.

Apparently, he was the designated stripper.

Her swelling belly was visible with the fabric gone.

Triton smiled and pressed his hand to cover the bump. He closed his eyes and chuckled. "You are doing very well, Emmy. There are two in there."

She swallowed nervously. "Whose are they?"

He grinned. "We won't know until

you are further along. This home has been crafted for you to keep you in comfort during your pregnancy. As you can't age while my mother's necklace is on, you will have to spend your pregnant time here on land."

She whispered. "Why can't I remain in the human world?"

"Ah, mistress, we want to continue to enjoy you, even if we have to slow down our attentions." He grinned. "You are ours, darling."

She shivered at the intensity in his dark eyes. Hands began to caress her back, ass, arms and breasts. She was urged into the shelter that they had arranged for her. It was an ancient temple styled with a wide bed in the centre. Fruit was piled high in a bowl, a bathing pool was bubbling away, and Davis explained the bathroom arrangement.

When they were all standing near the bed, she was given a light toga that left one breast bare and fell to mid-thigh.

Triton smiled. "You look lovely. I hope you have an uneventful gestation. We have been looking to swell our ranks, but no other woman has managed to survive our attentions."

She shivered at the memory. "I can't think of why."

The group chuckled as one.

Davis knelt and took her exposed nipple between his lips, sucking carefully to keep her from the deadly edges of his teeth.

Leson pressed his lips to her neck, and Triton was watching, his hand wrapped around the thick column of his cock, moving slowly.

As quickly as the clothing had come on, it was a whisper of fabric at her feet while she was held, stroked, fingers slid into her pussy and then worked into her ass. She panted and her cries echoed off the stone around her.

Every sound she made increased their frenzy. She screamed as she came and whimpered as their fingers continued to drive and twist into her.

Triton's cock was thick and shades darker than the surrounding skin. He moved his brother's hand aside and pushed into her opening. A whine of sound rippled out of her as she fought to relax around him. When she had managed to keep her body from going into full revolt, he gripped her hips and pulled her up and down on him in a slow rocking motion. He stood with his legs apart and pumped into her with jolting thrusts.

She was breathing easier as her body adjusted to the sheer girth of him, but when she felt someone coming up behind her and spreading something slick on her ass, she tensed.

Triton groaned, and her rear lover pressed into her, moving slowly and deliberately into her ass. The slight abrasion as he moved into her identified her invader as Davis.

She was too full as they jostled inside her stretched-open pussy and ass. She screamed as a wave of pleasure swept through her, and the sound electrified them into a frenzy of action. One withdrew and the other plunged in, rocking her back and forth with hard jolts.

Emmy's body reacted to the rough handling, and she teetered on the edge for a moment before Triton grunted and held her tight while Davis jackhammered into her ass until he let out a deep groan, pulled out and came against her lower back.

She collapsed against Triton, and the pressure on her clit had her shivering and twitching around him. She groaned softly, and he held her on him with one hand while he walked with her to the bed. To her nervous anticipation, he lay on his back with her over him. Another cock pressed for entrance, and a third pressed against her lips. She tasted salt and smelled musk as he pushed into her. Her eel lover, Leson, held her head as she sucked at him while one of the others used her ass.

Triton remained inside her, thickening again as the friction woke his cock. She blinked as Leson came with a choked sound, spewing cum down her throat. She choked but swallowed while he pulsed against her tongue.

Leson retreated when he was spent, and she felt the hard shove in her ass a moment before her lover shook.

Triton smiled slowly and thrust into her while another took the rear position.

They fucked her leisurely in turns until she collapsed on Triton. She woke in his arms, and he rolled over her and into her, thrusting deep and slow.

He smiled. "I can hardly wait until

you are back in the water and I can take all of you at once."

She shivered. It was a threat as much as a promise.

They fed her, clothed her, undressed her and fucked her. She lost track of the days, but she noted that they gentled their attentions when her belly started fighting back against the pressure.

Davis was giving her a back rub on the day that she went into labour. He kissed her quickly and carried her to the pool where they entered and exited her little temple.

In the water, Triton delivered his tentacle son three hours later, and Davis held the little shark man against him with a stunned grin on his face.

Emmy looked at the monsters that she had birthed and felt a profound sense of relief. They were alive, they were healthy, and she was done. Blood drained between her thighs, and she let herself fade away. The dream was over.

She woke up while Leson was wiping her body down, cleaning her from head to toe. Her belly was flat. "How long have I been out?"

Leson smiled. "A year. You were near death, so we petitioned our father to let us keep you. He agreed, but it has taken time for your immortality to take hold."

She raised her hands and noted the webbing in her hands. "What has happened to me?"

Leson smiled brightly at her. "You have been given the gift of the sea and the land. You can walk both with the same appearance. We can be with you for eternity."

She looked at him as she took inventory of her body. She felt the same for the most part, but when she searched with her hands, she found her gills, her feet were webbed, and her vision saw everything more clearly.

"Why?"

"You gave Triton a son. You gave our father grandsons. He is delighted with you and will be here in a few years to sample you for himself." Leson spoke as if there wasn't anything wrong with that.

She sat up, and her thighs slid together. "Has someone been fucking me?"

Leson smiled. "Of course. We are careful not to overuse you, but we have our needs."

She nodded and slowly got to her feet. Her skin was a pearly white, and her hair hung down over her breasts. "I think I would like to go for a swim."

Emmy didn't know what her plan was, but she suspected that she could get loose when she hit the open water. She simply had to find the open water.

She was nearly to the water's edge when her men rose up and crossed their arms.

Triton smiled grimly. "Where are you going?"

She could see that he read her intent. "I am just going for a swim."

"Good. We will all go, and then, you will be shackled in the grotto for a few decades. You are not escaping us, Emmy."

He extended his hand, and she took it, wrapped in his tentacled embrace as he sank beneath the surface with her pinned to him.

She was surrounded on all sides, and it was when she was shackled in the grotto that her mind slipped away with the thought... *How long is eternity anyway?*

Swipe Right

She giggled as he fondled her knee. How lucky had she been to get such a guy with the app? He was witty, charming and had a wicked sense of humour. She was having an amazing time.

"So, Molly, this house has been on the market for two decades. The original owner provided for the maintenance in a trust, but it ran out. The company has been trying to unload it since."

The huge and majestic mansion got larger until the sprawl took up the entire horizon.

"Why didn't they give it to a historical society?"

"No one will take it." Darryl smirked. "Would you like to come inside and look around?"

Molly could feel the innuendo in his invitation, but she didn't really mind. She was out to have some fun.

When they exited the car, he took her hand and hauled her toward the wide entryway. He used the lockbox and removed the key.

The doors swung wide, and Molly stepped inside.

Darryl whispered to her, "They say that the house hates the sound of angry voices. It raises the ghosts inside."

She felt a shiver that had nothing to do with the hand sliding inside her shirt and up her back. She stepped away. "You never said it was haunted."

He smiled. "If you are scared, I can hold your hand... or anything else you want me to grab."

She rolled her eyes and headed into

the house, curious and intent on following the draw that pulled her deeper and deeper into the maze of halls and walls.

Darryl pursued her and pinned her to the wall, kissing at her neck. "Come on, Molly. We have this entire palace to ourselves."

She chuckled and leaned her head to one side for a moment before pushing him away. "I don't think that I want to do that kind of a thing in this house. It feels disrespectful."

He snorted and pulled her closer. "Don't be a fucking tease."

She pushed him back and was about to scream at him when a new voice sounded.

"Get away from him, bitch." A blonde woman who had obviously been crying was standing in the doorway.

Molly froze when she realized that there was a gun pointing at her. "Uh, ma'am, he has me pinned to the wall. He has to move away."

Darryl held his hands out, and he stepped aside, leaving her in line for the barrel.

"Baby, you know that you haven't felt like doing it lately. Do you blame me for looking for some on the side?"

Molly felt the flame of fury in her body. "You said you were single. I asked you three times if you were single. You said you weren't seeing anyone. I am all up for fun, but this is messed up. I am out of here."

She stepped to the side and heard the sharp pop of the gun. Molly looked to one side, and the bookshelf she was next to had a bullet hole through the wood of the shelf. She stumbled back and everything went white.

Molly straightened, and she felt that time had passed. She was alone in the hall, and Darryl and his creepy girlfriend were nowhere to be seen.

She reached for her phone but couldn't find her purse. Ah well. She could head for the main road and hail a cab. It would take an hour to get there, but she could manage it.

A dark laugh rang through the halls. Molly froze.

She looked to where she remembered the door being, and she glanced around in confusion. The door was gone. Smooth wood was in its place.

"It seems your lover has left you here to your own devices." The rich voice spilled out of one of the chambers off to her left.

She followed the voice and found a man lounging in a deep chair, sipping a glass of brandy. "Do you know him?"

"He brings his conquests here, one at a time. We watch, but since nothing comes of it, we let him go."

"Let him go? Is he trespassing?"

"Oh, definitely, but he puts on a good show, so we tolerate him."

Molly stared, but she couldn't see into the shadows that disguised her conversational companion. "Do you know how I can get out of here?"

"Of course. The key is silence. No matter what you hear, see or feel, you cannot utter a sound. You may not even ask our names once the way out has begun. Silence is your key."

"I don't understand." She stared at him, and the air wavered around him.

"You don't have to understand; you just have to choose. Do you want to come out the other side, or do you want to shatter the world around you by uttering a sound? The choice is yours."

The world spun again, and Molly was in a long hallway. Doors lined the hall, and sideboards broke up the stark appearance of the wood and dark wallpaper. She stepped toward the door at the end of the hall when a door opened next to her.

Ignoring it was her plan, but as she tried to step forward, it was like being stuck in thick honey. She couldn't go forward. She couldn't go back. The open door was her only option.

She stared at her shoes while she decided. She could remain in the hall and shout her head off, but what would that get her?

The black pumps didn't give her any insight into what was going on, so she walked toward the open room.

The door swung shut behind her, and she jumped. Molly turned and tried to open the door, but the lock wouldn't turn in her hand.

She felt a hand stroke her spine, and she whirled to look at the person touching her, but there was no one.

Shivering in confusion, she walked past a low couch and toward a desk where a piece of paper was lying in the centre of the glossy mahogany.

Elbows on the table and lean forward, ass out. Don't move and don't make a sound.

Molly stood upright and walked around to the door and tried it again. She wasn't going to play whatever sick game was taking place here. She made a fist and pounded on the door.

A hand grabbed her arm and turned her around. She had a moment to take in his sharp and handsome features before he kissed her, stroking his tongue between her lips with the confidence of a man who knew she wasn't going to bite.

He pressed her to the door and lifted her, holding her with his pelvis, and the ridge of his erection was enticing. She shivered and returned his kiss. She had come out that night wanting a little fun, and he seemed willing to give it to her. As he leaned away, she opened her lips, but he pressed a finger to her mouth.

To her surprise, he nodded toward the desk and winked. A moment later, he disappeared.

She began to shake and felt a hand at the base of her spine, moving in a slow circle.

He wasn't real, right? So she could bend over the desk, and all she would do was embarrass herself. If this wasn't real, she would just have to deal with her subconscious at a later date.

Sticking her ass the air in front of a webcam wasn't the worst thing she had ever done. At least she got to keep her clothing on.

At this point, the webcam was all she could think of. She called herself seventeen kinds of stupid while she walked over to the desk, and when she had settled her forearms against the smooth wood, she heard a chuckle that was so soft as to be nearly silent.

She heard, rather than saw, the steps behind her. She didn't turn around. She kept her face toward the message on the paper.

The touch on her backside was warm, and he didn't hesitate. Both hands cupped her buttocks and massaged them with strong motions.

Molly opened her mouth and would have gasped, but she remembered what had been said, and she closed her jaws with a snap.

The fingers gripped her butt, and she glanced behind her, shocked to see no one there. A hand left her backside and held her head, turning her forward.

She could feel him, could feel the heat of his thighs against the back of her skirt. He wasn't there. He really wasn't there. She closed her eyes as he ran his hands over her ass for a few more minutes before he flipped her skirt up and hooked the waistband of her panties, pulling the small barrier down her thighs.

The feeling of lips on her ass made her jump, and she tried to turn to face him, but he used his hand on her once again. He held her head forward until she stopped resisting and resumed his delicate attentions to the globes of her butt.

Whoever—whatever—was kissing her, he really liked her ass. It sent a shudder through her when she guessed at what would come next.

Kinky games were her favourite part of the dating app. She could have a guy for a night and then move on to the next with no worries about judgment or repeat performances. While she wasn't a fan of how it started, she was enjoying the kink that Darryl had brought her to.

She would worry about how they managed the effects later. For now, she was getting hot.

She kept her eyes closed as fingers slid up and down the seam of her ass. When the rough fingertips circled her slit, she jumped a little. He held her down with a hand to her spine and slid one digit into her.

Molly's face was hot. She knew how wet she was. Hide and seek and blindfolds were her favourite games. This was a neat twist on her old favourites.

He moved his hand and thrust another finger into her. She bit her lip and arched her back. The third finger was a tight fit, but she was wet enough that it still went in.

She flexed her hands on the wood and tried to dig her nails into the polished surface.

The hand thrust in and out, a few inches of motion that had her shaking with the need to cum.

Molly tightened around his fingers and focused on sending herself over the edge.

He pulled his fingers away and fit the head of his cock against her.

The hot, hard shaft fit into her, and the girth stretched her just enough to be on the uncomfortable side. With a few thrusts, the friction had her back on the edge, and she drew her nails down the wood as she opened her mouth in a silent scream.

She could still feel her pussy clenching around him when his fingers pressed against the entrance to her ass. Unless she missed it, he hadn't cum, and he did have that fascination for her butt. He wasn't done yet.

Instead of being an idiot and trying to use her own moisture as lube, he rubbed something thick and slick into her asshole. His fingers began to loosen her next, and when she had taken two of his digits he pulled them out before he pressed his cock into her, holding her hips and sliding into her, inch by inch.

She pushed back against him, wincing at the ache and burn that he was inflicting, but loving the dark pleasure that was rippling through her.

The moment she could feel his balls against her thighs and the prickle of hair against her skin, he started moving with slow and easy motions that built in ferocity over long minutes until he was hammering at her and she was bracing herself on the desk for support.

He reached beneath her and gripped her breasts, squeezing and kneading at her until she bucked back against him again as a shivering orgasm ran through her.

He jerked his hips into her, and she guessed at the cum shooting inside her. When he pulled out, a dribble trailed down the back of her thighs. She held still, her hands braced on the table and sweat dripping from her skin.

He placed a kiss on her left buttock, slid her panties back into place and smoothed her skirt back over her butt. She gasped and throbbed where he had been inside her, and when her vision cleared, she looked down at the note.

Walk down the hall and go to the next room. You can rest there. Don't say a word.

She straightened and could feel the wetness seeping out of her. Her ass was still tight, but she trusted that it would be a mess when it came time to clean up.

Molly looked around, and the door was open. She moved stiffly and carefully out the door and down the hall until she ran into the heavy and impassible air again. The door that was open beckoned her in.

She heard the sound of running water and followed it to the bathroom, where a soaker tub was filling with warm water and a mound of bubbles.

The invitation was clear, and she was sticky and slick enough to give in. Her clothing hit the floor in an untidy heap. She flicked her panties away so that they wouldn't get her dress wet, though the dress was soaked with sweat and the bra was no better.

Her heels were knocked over and abandoned as she stepped into the bath. The heat told her where the abrasions were, and she settled in for a long soak. Morning would be soon enough for her to hike to the main road. Walking around in the dark was dangerous.

She settled back and relaxed until the water was tepid. Every inch of her had been scrubbed clean, and she could almost think that she had imagined the previous encounter. She would have if her clothing hadn't disappeared to be replaced by a long muslin gown hanging from the door.

She dried off with super-soft linen

and hung it up carefully. The gown was obviously for her, so she slipped it on and removed the clip that kept her hair off her face. The bed was covered with lace, and one side of the bedding was turned down in invitation. Molly didn't want to be rude, so she slipped into the envelope prepared for her and settled against the pillows.

She was nearly asleep when she felt a body pressing against hers under the blankets. She smiled slightly and burrowed back against him.

Molly drifted in and out of an alert mode as his hands went on a slow exploration of her body. She opened her mouth to comment on his previous knowledge of her, but he pressed his fingers to her lips.

She licked at the fingers and sucked them into her mouth. He quivered against her back and burrowed beneath the bedding.

She wasn't sure what he was up to until he arranged her on her back and slowly lifted the edge of her nightgown as he kissed his way up to her sex.

She felt his breath on her before he applied his mouth to her slit with delicate ferocity. He was careful but savage as he worked her body into moving against his tongue.

She pressed her hand to her mouth as she soared toward release. Her first encounter had primed her, and now, she was up for an escalation of activity. Her hands gripped the pillow under her head as she gritted her teeth when her senses flew apart. Fire ran through her limbs, and her body pulsed around his tongue.

Molly was breathing hard, her body coated in sweat again as she settled against the sheets under the coverlet.

The man under the covers moved slowly up her body. She assumed he was going to slide into her, but instead, he took her left nipple between his teeth and bit carefully.

Her hand slammed over her mouth again as he moved from breast to breast, biting, sucking, nibbling and then starting all over.

Her senses were in overdrive. The dark of the room must have happened while she was dozing. She looked under the blanket, but all she could see was the unending darkness of the room around her.

He started to knead at her breasts as he sucked, and she bit her lip. She had always enjoyed rough handling. She pressed up toward her bed companion and rolled her hips against him.

The feel of his smile against the fabric that stuck to her from the wet of his mouth was triumphant.

He continued to play with her breasts for another ten minutes while she ground her hips against him.

She would have begged, but she was supposed to remain quiet. She let go of the pillow and threaded her fingers through his hair, pulling him away from her breasts for a kiss. His lips and tongue were surprisingly cool for the heated impact they had on her breasts.

She could taste the tang of herself in his mouth, but his own flavour was elusive. He broke the kiss, and a heartbeat later, she was alone. The blankets collapsed on her, and the only proof he had ever been there was the wet marks on her chest. The damp rings that his mouth had left were proof that she hadn't imagined him.

Her body was throbbing, and she debated what to do. She could get up and stumble around in the dark or stay in bed, throbbing and frustrated.

With all of the weirdness going on, she chose to remain in bed. She wouldn't sleep, and her clit was too tender to touch, so she just lay there and waited for light.

Some sick son of a bitch had changed her clothing while she slept. The satiny gown and slippers belonged in a historical re-enactment. She felt something in her hair and found a ribbon tied in a bow on top of her head. She was someone's dress-up doll.

The mirror in the corner showed her that she looked as dorky as she felt. All she needed was Mr. Darcy and the illusion would be complete. She turned from side to side. Her boobs took up the entire top of the empire waistline. The flow of the dress just hinted at the curve of her hip.

It was very pretty, but it wasn't her normal style. She liked things from this century, flowy and above the knee.

As she turned, she had one silent question. *How did they get a corset on*

---

me in my sleep?

It was definitely a two-man job.

She looked like a doll, but her clothing was nowhere to be seen. She didn't have an option if she wanted to make her way out.

The fabric slippers hissed lightly on the polished wood as she walked through the bedroom and out to the hall. When the force stopped her again, she was next to a sideboard. It was peculiar. She looked to the next door, but it was closed and the ones behind her had ceased to appear in the hallway.

She was going to ask what was going on, but shadows filled the hall until the sideboard was the only spot of light.

Molly moved to the side as the shadows pushed at her. She backed against the wood, and she waited for whatever happened next.

Her suitor came out of the shadows, wearing a flowing black shirt and indecently tight pants that were tucked into knee-high boots.

He smiled slowly and bowed right in front of her before standing upright again. She reached up and pressed a finger to his lips and one to her own. He smiled and took her digit into his mouth, swirling his tongue around it.

Her decorum and normally shy demeanour had gone with her underwear. She was being offered a chance to enjoy herself, and the men she was meeting didn't seem to be particularly chatty. She was on the pill and had full medical coverage. She was going to take advantage of what was on offer.

The swirling warmth of his tongue showed teasing dexterity and a willingness to use it.

She pulled her finger free with a soft pop.

He wrapped an arm around her, pulling her tightly against his body. He was hard all over, but the ridge of his erection was exceptionally enticing.

He kissed the side of her neck and gnawed gently. Molly tilted her head to the side and wrapped the dangling length of his cravat in her hands, pulling him toward her. He sucked strongly at her skin, and she clenched her thighs together. Her neck was an underutilized erogenous zone, and just the stroking of his lips and tongue were having a definite effect.

She wanted to sigh and moan and do all of the normal things that she did when she was excited, but she had to keep quiet or the game would end.

She really didn't want the game to end.

He lifted her up and set her down on the sideboard. He curled his hands in the top of her modest gown and pulled sharply. She inhaled, and her breasts nearly broke the confines of the corset.

Her lover smiled and stroked the soft surface of the mounds, easing one finger inside to stroke her nipple.

He scratched gently at the left and then the right. She licked her lips and stared into his dark eyes as the light touches caused her pussy to clench in eagerness.

He stepped toward her and used both hands to undo the clasp at the top of the corset. The rest of it remained tight on her ribs. He arranged her breasts to his satisfaction with her nipples peeping at the edge of the corset. When the image was what he wanted, he stroked his hands down her boned waist and slid down her thighs to her knees. He eased her legs apart and stepped into the vee.

He pressed his lips to the hollow between her breasts as he gathered the skirt above her hips, and he pulled her forward until she was lined up with his groin. He slid his hand between them and rubbed three fingers against her.

The slick moisture that her body was producing coated his fingers. She blushed when she realized that he was watching her as he fingered her.

She jolted as he circled his fingers around her outer lips, pressing against her clit until she closed her eyes against the focused viewing. Molly felt him pry her hand loose and press it against the wood beside her. She released the cravat with her other hand and braced herself back.

When she opened her eyes, he was smiling and freeing his cock from the button front of his trousers. He pressed in close, and the fleeting view of his erection disappeared under the froth of her skirts. He wrapped his arm around her and lifted her, angling her so that he could slide in.

The angle was hard, and the fit was tight. He didn't wait. He bounced her on him, and she bit her lip until it bled to keep from crying out.

His hips hammered upward, and she stiffened when the orgasm struck. He paused with her fully on him, their bodies so tight that they were nearly one person. When her inner caress finally spiralled to a halt, he started to move inside her once again.

The sudden jolts shook her breasts, and that seemed to be what he was after, because he drove into her over and over until she felt bruised. Her second climax was hard, and he kept fucking her until his own body gave in. He shuddered, kissed her breasts and disappeared so suddenly that she nearly fell.

The lights came on, and the second to last door swung open in invitation. Molly lay back on the sideboard and caught her breath. Fucking in a corset was harder than it looked.

She put on the shoe that she had lost

during the pummelling and wandered down the hall to the open door when she felt she was ready.

She could feel the sun and the breezes the moment she stepped through the doorway. The weird thing was that she couldn't see it.

The room was a sitting room with a series of chairs in a semi-circle. There were cocktails on the small occasional tables next to the chairs, and it reminded her that she wasn't hungry or thirsty. It was peculiar, as she should have had to pee at least once since this whole thing began.

Invisible hands stroked her hair, pulling the ribbon free. Her dress was unfastened and slipped from her shoulders. She was left standing in the chemise and corset.

It felt like two sets of hands slowly stripped her to the skin. Her laces were undone, and the corset was loosened.

The air touching her all over made her shiver.

She was left alone, wearing only her slippers.

One by one, the seven chairs were occupied. Men appeared out of mist and settled next to their beverages of choice.

She recognized the first man from the study. His clothing was modern-dress casual. He raised his glass to her and looked her over.

She enjoyed the fascinated attention for about three minutes, and then, she wanted her normal clothing back.

Molly was amazed to find herself wearing jeans, a t-shirt and sneakers. She looked down in surprise, and the men gave rueful smiles.

She opened her mouth to speak, and they held their fingers to their lips as one. Without speaking, they pointed out the door and to the last doorway in the hall.

Wearing comfortably normal clothing, she headed for the doorway, and here was the wind and sunlight. She had gone from inside to outside in a heartbeat. The door behind her remained open.

"You can speak now. Nothing will happen." The man she had first met was standing next to her.

"Where are we?"

He pointed to the gathering a few yards away. "We are at your funeral. We have not had a woman die within our walls before. We made every effort to keep your soul with us while your body died. I hope that we made your passing painless."

She stared at him. "I am dead?"

"You began to die the moment that the bullet passed through you, and we caught your soul before it could leave the house. While they were treating you and trying to keep you alive, we had to keep your soul busy. One word would have put you back in your body and we would have lost our chance."

Molly stared at him. "Your chance?"

"To have a female companion here at the house. We have died decades apart and all have differing desires in the bedroom. You seem to have an open mind and a willingness to experiment."

She shivered at the thought of further experimentation. "You let me die just to have a fuck buddy?"

He shook his dark head. "You were dying anyway. We just diverted you on the way to your final resting place."

Molly remembered something that Darryl had said. "Won't the house be sold?"

"No. It remains in a trust to an ancient group of paranormal investigators. They come and speak with us now and then. In exchange for our cooperation, they put the house up for sale now and then to bring in some contemporaries so that we can keep abreast of the living world.”

“Why don’t the investigators tell you what you need?”

“They are too fixated on the past.” He shrugged. “So, we have them bring the modern world to us.”

“Those are my parents. So… she shot me?”

“Yes. She struck near your heart, and we pulled you out. It is disconcerting to see one’s dying body.” He took her hand. “If it makes you feel better, she is being charged for your murder. Her companion as well. He liked to taunt her into jealous fits. You were just the means to the end.”

Molly looked at him. “You have seen them before.”

“Three times in the same week. He would lure a woman with him, his woman would attack and they would have sex while the newcomer ran for safety. Yours was the first time that she brought a pistol."

"Who are you?"

"I am Gerald. I am the most recent addition to the house. Well, aside from you. You are the newest haunt to our home."

She blushed and looked down at their hands. "What was with all the sex?"

He laughed, and she looked up at him. He was grinning. "We are men, though we no longer walk the world. Having a woman at our disposal after so many years was an opportunity we did not want to miss."

She covered her eyes with her free hand and groaned. She should have felt something for the mourners who wailed that she was gone too soon, for her parents who watched her casket being lowered into the soil. There was no place in her for grief. She had moved beyond her body, and there was so much more to do.

Molly looked down at her casual attire and changed it to something a little more feminine with the classic draping of ancient Greece.

He pulled her up against him and smiled. "How did you know? The classics are my favourite."

Her hair pulled up into a loose arrangement, and she pulled his head down for a kiss.

He escorted her back into the house via the open doorway, and as it closed behind her; he disappeared in a flash.

Molly clutched her chest as agony screamed through her.

Darryl was shouting, "Amy, what did you do?"

The woman was staring at the gun. "It went off. It just went off. I wasn't even holding the trigger."

Molly tried to speak and blood caught in her throat. No words emerged, only gurgling.

The other two ran, and Molly saw her phone come out of her tiny purse where 911 was dialled. She watched the phone float to the floor as seven shimmering figures surrounded her.

Gerald's voice whispered in her ear, "We said you couldn't speak. We didn't want to say why. See you in a few minutes, darling. We have centuries of playtime lined up."

She stared at the spectral faces watching her as she waited for the ambulance to show up before she died. Molly felt herself leaving her body as the police came through the door.

"Damn it! What was all that stuff before if I wasn't dead yet?" Molly put her hands on her hips and glared at the men around her.

Gerald chuckled. "We just wanted to make sure that you didn't enter the light. This place is so much more fun. We promise to keep you entertained."

A man she didn't remember seeing before stepped forward. She would have remembered him; he was built like an ox.

"It seems that you have a penchant for cursing, little miss. That means you are in dire need of discipline. Come here; I am going to take you over my knee."

She looked at him and stepped back, but two of the others cut off her escape route. He grabbed her and literally tucked her under his arm while he walked to a chair, sat down and settled her over his knees.

He lifted her skirt up and tucked it over her back then pulled her panties down to expose all of her to his hand. The first smack drove all thought out of her head.

The second smack was distracting, because the other six had formed a semi-circle around her with their chairs while she was spanked, and through the spectral veil, she watched the ambulance attendants work on her.

It was a death that lacked dignity, but she had centuries to work out a way to get her revenge.

Cross Country

Sea huffed and tried to keep up with her group. She really didn't want to be here, but her friends had bullied her into coming with them to round out their number. If she weren't there, they wouldn't have gotten the discount on the guide.

There was nothing like being used for your ability to be a warm body.

She was last in line again and shuffled along in the trail of the man ahead of her. The group was getting further away again, and she fought to keep up.

That night, they were going to spend the evening at a lodge prepared for their group, and the next day, they would return to the base camp. Lea was counting the minutes until she was out of the snow pants and into her car.

She mindlessly shuffled ahead, taking stock of the sweat on her skin as well as the ache in her butt. She fell a lot.

The snowy world around her was beautiful, but the laughter from the group up ahead wrecked the promise of silence that the white world was giving her.

She cruised into a clearing with calls of, "There she is." And "Finally. Lea, what kept you?"

She flipped them the bird and set her poles so she could drop her pack and get her thermos out.

She looked around, found a spot, released her skis and headed over to a snow-covered log.

Lea watched the couples interacting, and she fought the urge to groan. Although Samantha had been married for three years, she was trying to bat her lashes at the guide and get him to help her form.

Lea shook up her soup and poured a measure of it into her cup. She sipped at it slowly while the guide moved around the group to brief them on what was happening next.

When it was her turn, Brady brushed the snow off the log and settled down next to her. He leaned over. "You are miserable, aren't you?"

She made a face. "Yup. Just counting the hours."

"Why are you here? You don't seem the type to make it this deep into the woods."

Lea chuckled. "I am not, but I promised myself that I wouldn't pass up any opportunity to try something new. This is the something new, and I am trying it. I like the forest, though."

He grinned. "Excellent. That is half

the battle. Well, we are heading downhill for a bit, so expect to go fast or bite the dust. Don't be afraid to shout out if you go down."

Lea sighed. "You will be too far up to hear me. I fall over with amazing stealth."

He smiled. "Eat something else before we go. You are burning more calories than you think."

"Yes, sir. Whatever you say, Brady."

He winked and got to his feet. "Call me sir."

She watched him walk away; his outdoor clothing masked what she guessed was an impressive physique. He certainly looked like he had a lot of stamina.

She was still watching him walk away when he turned and winked at her. Her cheeks flared with a blush. Damn, he had caught her looking at his ass.

They were an hour into the afternoon

trek when Lea saw the man in front of her dip over a ledge and head down a hill. By the time she got to the top, he whooshed around the corner, leaving her alone.

Lea watched her skis bend and teeter at the edge of the hill. Her knees wobbled as she eased forward, and before she could change her mind, she was over the edge, bending low and trying not to die.

She went down the hill, made her own track and kept going straight through the brush. She squeaked as the leaves slapped her skin, and she continued further and further downhill. In a panic, she managed to stop herself in a wide sprawl. Why was it that the one time she needed to fall over, she cruised for what felt like miles?

Chunks of snow had made it up her jacket and crept into her snow pants during her slide. The icy trickle ran down her inner thigh as she unclipped her skis and headed back to retrieve her poles from whatever tree had grabbed them on her way down.

Lea looked up when the first fat flake of snow landed on her nose. "Fuck."

She followed her trail on foot, grabbing one pole at a time and moved quickly when she noticed that the path was being obliterated by the snow. Wind picked up and blew over her trail. She wanted to scream, but she moved faster, trying to keep an eye on the path she had taken to get to her current location.

Snow came down, and the wind swirled it, blinding her until she had no idea which way she was going. Tears froze onto her lashes as she continued hiking. She dropped her skis and used her poles to help her fight through the bush.

An hour later, her legs were burning and she was calling herself seventeen kinds of stupid. The sun was setting soon, and she needed to find shelter if she wasn't going to turn into a sad story. She started looking for a place to wait out the snow.

The crisp air had lost its allure, and it was only when she saw a stone gash in a low hill that she felt she had a chance. Bat caves might be diseased, but most of what they carried was curable, and those little bodies gave off a lot of heat. She was willing to risk bats.

The exposed stone that wasn't holding onto the snow told her it was warmer than the surrounding area. That was good as well. She kept her poles with her as she crept toward the crevice. The warmer air didn't have the stench of dung, so she eased inside and felt a flutter of hope that she wouldn't die in the frozen forest.

In the morning, she could orient herself and head south to the parking lot and her car. She had a compass, but with the fading light, she didn't have time to get back to her vehicle.

If she had a map or directions, she would have tried for the cabin, but that wasn't something that she had been offered, and she had been too shy to insist on a copy.

The warm air inside the cave was moist, and she followed the current through twists and turns to a wide pool that stretched off into the darkness.

The steam coming off the water had formed a slick surface on the stone, so she moved carefully around the heat source and tried not to consider herself lucky.

The humidity would soak into her suit and freeze her to death the next day. She had to take steps to protect her outerwear.

With a deep sigh, she emptied the contents of her pack onto the slick stone and then peeled off her ski suit, stuffing it into the protection of her pack. At least she wouldn't be putting on a sodden mess the next day.

Looking down at her inner layer, she made a decision. She stripped down to the thin thermal underwear and put the rest of her clothing in the pack with the compressed suit.

The cave was dark, but an odd glow was coming up from the depths of the water. With the absolute darkness in the shadows, the light actually made the room comfortable, if a little creepy.

Lea ate one of the granola bars in her pack and finished the soup before scooting to the highest and driest edge she could find. She checked the time on her phone, noted that there were still no bars and put it to sleep to save the battery. She would use the light in the morning to find her way out.

The puff of her pack was her pillow,

and she settled against it to sleep.

She smiled in the darkness. "Nothing like cross-country skiing for a good night's sleep."

Her sarcasm kept her from crying.

Someone was in his territory. He lifted his head to sniff and followed the light, feminine scent toward the hot spring.

The taste of her fear hung in the air, and it made him hesitate. When he stood in the shadows and watched her settling in to sleep next to the sedating spring, he had to admire her thinking with her placement. She was as dry as she could get, but if he left her there, she would not get up. The gases given off by the spring were toxic to mammals over a period of hours. The beasts knew enough to keep clear of this place.

He thought about it for a few heart-beats and watched as her breathing slowed. He had to get her, or she would not wake up.

He moved around the pool and caught her up, lifting her and cradling her against his chest while grabbing her pack in one motion.

His wide, heavy feet were silent as he stepped around the pool and retreated to the shadows where the access to his shelter was. The storm outside was going to take days. He was going to have something for his guest to eat.

He settled her in his sleeping pallet and headed outside to find some food before it all went to ground.

Lea turned and felt softness all around her. The sound of the water was gone, and she was in deep shadows where a small glow was the only light source.

She chalked it up to being half awake and settled back into sleep.

Lea felt, more than heard, that she was not alone. There was also the tang of blood in the air. That woke her up completely.

A huge, shadowy figure was in the corner, and the sound of ripping flesh was distinctly audible. Lea shivered. This was not where she had gone to sleep.

Her pack was a few feet away, and she knew it wasn't a dream. Her imagination never included scents of musk and blood when she dreamed.

She must have made a sound, because the shadow paused and slowly turned toward her.

She covered her mouth with her hand as she swallowed her scream. *Has to be a dream, has to be a dream, a dream, a dream.*

Bigfoot was real, covered with blood and had a chunk of raw meat in his hand.

She held perfectly still, and he put the meat on a stick and parked it over the small fire in the corner of the room. He calmly dealt with the rest of the carcass, carrying it to the next room.

She was shaking with fear.

He glanced at her, huffed and passed her, covered with blood. She couldn't see what was in the shadows, but he disappeared.

The moment he was out of her sight, she ran to the exit where he had taken the deer. Her body felt heavy, jerky. A thick animal pelt hung from the top of the wall, and as she pushed it aside, she was wrapped in frozen hell. Different carcasses were embedded in the walls. Ice was forming on the fresh meat and there were two fully clothed human bodies on the far side. There was no way out of this room.

A huff sounded behind her, and she turned slowly to see the eight-foot beast-man looking at her. He was damp and the fur on his torso frosted as she stared at him.

He let out another huff and wrapped an arm around her, pulling her against him and out of the cold room.

She shivered as his hand covered her back. He urged her back into the warmth of the room she had woken in, and the blood had been cleaned up from the butchering spot. He was very fast.

The meat was starting to sizzle over the fire, and when he had her coaxed back into the fur-lined nest, she watched him twist the stick so that the other side began to warm.

With his domestic duties completed, he walked over to her.

She took in the rich brown fur, the huge dark eyes in the ugly and vaguely human face.

He pointed to the frozen room and grunted out with some difficulty. "Frozen. Death."

He pointed to the exit he had used to bathe. "Water. Death for people. You sleep. You dead."

He was making a lot of effort to speak, and she understood against her own better judgment.

"I can just go."

He shook his huge head. "Storm. Days."

She blinked in surprise. "What?"

"Not safe. Storm days. You die."

Days?

She shrank back while her mind spun. "Why save me? There are two dead men in the cave."

A bright smile came into his huge eyes. "They slept. They died. You slept and alive. Very soft."

She blinked at the warmth in his tone, forced around the fangs that were visible when he spoke.

It was obvious that communication was difficult, so she eased toward him. "I am in your bed. You need it more than I do."

He grunted. "Stay. We share."

She wasn't quite sure what he meant until he moved toward her, crowding her against the wall. He pulled her against him and rolled so that she was watching the small flames that were cooking her meal. She was pretty sure it was for her, as his teeth had shown he was more than capable of going directly to the source.

One of his huge hands was around her ribs with a thumb between her breasts. The other was around her hips. He let out a happy sound and pulled her in until the soft fur on his body was nestled against her back.

Lea shivered nervously, but it soon became obvious that he was willing to leave her on her own. He wanted to sleep.

His chin was on top of her head, and she fought the slow rhythm of his breathing. It was no use, she was still drowsy, and he took her with him into sleep.

The smell of food woke her, and to her shock, her bedmate was crouched by the fire, turning the meat.

Lea smiled slightly. Bigfoot had bed-head.

She sat up as he pulled the meat away from the fire. It looked fully cooked, which could only mean she had been out for hours.

He huffed when he saw her sitting up and beckoned her in close. With his long fingers, he peeled off strands of meat and offered them to her.

She was hungry, but taking the meat from his hands seemed weirdly ritualistic. It was plain but hot, and she collected all the pieces from him, slowly nibbling until hunger overcame manners.

She consumed the portion and licked her lips. "I am guessing that the water isn't safe."

He huffed again and walked to the wall near the spring. He brought back a leather skin that sloshed. He carefully enunciated, "Snow."

She smiled and found the opening, drinking carefully but keeping one eye on her host.

"Now I need to ask about where I can... uh... relieve myself?"

He made another huffing noise and beckoned her to follow him. He took her through a hall, and she could feel the heat from the spring. A deep alcove had a small waterfall and a wide pit below it.

He pointed, and it was instruction enough. He lumbered back down the tunnel, but she could feel him waiting for her.

She had to strip from the waist down to crouch without soaking her clothing, and after cleaning up in the warm waterfall, she tried to tug the insulated Lycra back into place over skin that wasn't co-operating.

She washed her hands and soaked her head, trying to clear it. With wet hair and feeling a little more in control of her body, she returned to her host.

He blinked his eyes slowly when she came around the corner. The dim light must have been enough for him. He trailed his fingers down her wet hair and down to where her nipples were straining at the fabric from the cold and damp.

A tiny zing of pleasure went through her at the touch. She moved back, and he huffed, wrapping a hand behind her and pulling her back into the living area.

Lea didn't fight him. He had torn a deer limb from limb with his bare hands. Her safety and survival was at his whim.

For all of her modern-woman philosophies, she didn't think she would have to worry about him wrecking her reputation in the real world, so as long as doing what he wanted didn't hurt her, she would go along with him.

No one would ever believe her anyway.

He stood her next to the nest of furs and knelt in front of her. He tugged at her clothing. "Go."

She glanced between his thighs and saw something twitching. "Can't I just..." She made a motion toward his groin.

He pulled at her shirt again. "Go."

Lea pulled her shirt off and then bent to peel her leggings away. Her bending took her perilously close to his rising cock, and her senses went into overdrive, taking in the heat coming from his body and the salty, musky scent that came to greet her. It had the wild smell of forest loam in the autumn, a strangely specific scent, but that was what she smelled.

The leggings were folded carefully and set aside with the shirt, and she stood with her damp hair and naked skin.

He made a low grumble and stroked the pink tips of her breasts. He was gentle and careful, like she was a kitten.

The skin of his fingers was a dark brown with a grey undertone, like the footpad of an animal. He was incredibly careful as he slowly flicked her nipples until they ached.

She shivered and he huffed again. His huge head approached her breast, and instead of opening his jaws to taste her, he reached out with a wide, flat tongue and scraped it along her skin.

"Ohmygod." The rasp was hot, wet and woke all of her nerves under her skin. She had always been indifferent to guys playing with her breasts during sex, but they didn't have a tongue as large as her palm. The force of his licking lifted one mound, and it bounced down when he reached the apex. He continued the licking over and over until she was weak in the knees and could smell her own heat.

Her clit throbbed, and the evidence of liquid invitation made her clench her thighs together.

He continued to lap at her until her breasts were red and tingled wildly.

She was surprised to find her hands wrapped around his head, keeping him where she wanted him. Embarrassed, she pulled her hands away, and he shifted his grip as well.

He slid one long finger between her thighs, rubbing in the slick honey she was producing. He grazed her clit, and she collapsed against him while her body throbbed and tried to grab at the cock inside her that wasn't there. She felt hollow, empty, and she wanted more.

He held her, and when she was upright again, he lifted his gleaming finger, and he licked it slowly. A deep growl left his throat, and he bent nearly to the ground, pulling her legs apart and snaking his tongue between her thighs.

She shuddered and gripped his head for balance as she closed her eyes, and the heat of his tongue rasped against her with slow, patient strokes.

When her knees gave way again, he caught her and gently laid her down on the furs. He didn't stop licking her; he worked his tongue against her until she was swollen, wet and desperately wanted something inside her.

Her hips rose and fell against his mouth, trying to get his tongue to do more than lap at her cream. She sighed in relief when he burrowed his tongue against her, pushing inside until she felt full and her entry was clenching around him. A low moan broke from her throat as a second wave of pleasure swept through her, letting her body follow its instincts without her thinking. She could think later. Right then, she wanted to feel.

He pulled his tongue out of her and licked his lips. His flattened nostrils flared as he slid a finger into her.

The rough pad of his finger caressed her, searching inside her as it delved deep. A low grunt sounded when he had gone as far as he could. She could feel her aftershocks fluttering around him.

He pulled out and had another finger join the first, stretching her. The process was slow, and she was sheened with sweat when the third finger joined the first two. He never went all the way to the base again, merely worked to gain her full opening for him.

Her flesh ached as he stretched her with the same delicate care that he had shown when he first touched her.

When her body gave him some sort of signal, he pulled his fingers free of her, sucked them clean, and then, he rose on his knees.

He flipped her and lifted her up so that her buttocks were presented to him, her slit wet and throbbing. She could feel his silky hair against her thighs as he moved over her, and she breathed in and out, keeping calm as he fit himself to her.

She braced herself on her forearms as he pressed into her, his cock as hot as his tongue, but infinitely stronger. She could feel her flesh giving way to his as he took up occupancy within her. She shuddered and pushed back onto him. It made his entry easier, and he stopped just before the aching stretch turned to pain.

Lea dug her hands into the furs and held on as he withdrew to slide into her again. There was a strange ring of impact around his cock when he thrust in, and a quick glance back showed her that he was gripping his erection with two fingers in an effort to keep from driving too deep.

Her appreciation was lost in a gasp as he surged into her, and he took up a frenzied beat that she had to brace against. Her sensitized breasts rubbed against the fur beneath her and her thighs were pressed by the fur on the back of his hands where he was holding himself. Flames were lit on either end of her body, and they worked toward the centre.

A few minutes of frenzied pounding and he let out a roar that echoed off the stone walls and rang in her ears. She could actually *feel* the jets of cum inside her.

His arms slammed down on either side of her as he caught his breath. He surrounded her, and he was still thick inside her. He wrapped one arm around her and held her belly as he took them both to their sides. He gave a slow shift of his hips that moved his receding length inside her, and she shivered, still close to release.

He licked at her neck and bit carefully while he stroked her clit. She shivered as his jaws deliberately broke skin, but the pain was enough to trigger her orgasm, and she fought to keep herself still.

When her channel randomly clasped his cock, he released her shoulder and licked at the wounds. She felt a deep lethargy run through her, and she dozed.

Warm water surrounded her as he bathed her in the pool he said was toxic.

He grunted when she flailed for freedom and slowly got out of the water after she did. He shook himself like a large dog, and the comparison made her smile while she took a look at her body.

There should have been more of an obvious mark than the slight reddening of skin. Lea mentally snorted as she thought about it. What was she going to have—a *Bigfoot was here* tattoo?

With his fur lightly damp, he held his hand to her. She reached up, and he helped her to her feet before lifting her and cuddling her against his chest.

Another chunk of meat was on the fire, and she was wondering how long she had been out.

He settled her back in the nest of furs. It had been rearranged. There was no sign of the sweat and cum that should have stained the fur. How long had she been asleep?

She pointed up. "Is the storm still there?"

He nodded. "One day left."

She nodded and stretched, trying to get the kinks out of her thighs. She stopped when she noticed he was watching her. "Sorry."

He reached out and stroked the curve of her hip. "Name?"

She blushed. "Lea."

He grunted and huffed before turning the meat. When dinner was attended to, he returned to her and joined her in the nest, curling around her and nuzzling her hair.

She heard him say softly, "Lea."

She rested with him until he brought his tongue into play again, licking his way down her spine before he flipped her to her back and burrowed between her thighs again.

Lea groaned and arched as he slid his tongue straight into her, priming her for him. When she was on the edge of release, he shifted his position and pressed his cock against her, moving to cover her nearly completely.

He wrapped his cock with one hand and pressed the sharp-tipped member into her, shoving deeply with one thrust.

Her lungs let out a whoosh of air as he went deep on the first thrust, but she soon was moving with him, wrapping her legs around his hips as he leaned down to brush her body with his fur.

Her nipples loved the friction, and she leaned into him, craving more as he fucked her to the edge of sanity before finally taking her over with him.

He shoved deep, and she yowled in pain when he hit her cervix, but he quickly moved to circle her clit rapidly until her orgasm kicked in, bringing the endorphins with it.

He backed up and bucked his hips in a flurry of short jabs that culminated in a low and drawn-out grunt.

The jetting inside her was unmistakable once again.

She watched the dazed look leave his face, and he smiled at her, the fangs clearly exposed. He leaned forward and nuzzled his cheek to hers. "Lea."

Lea was only too happy to escape into sleep once again.

Waking in the woods to hear her name being called, Lea looked down and found her body clad in all the layers she remembered from before the snowfall.

"I'm here!" She cleared her throat and shouted again, getting to her feet and brushing snow free of her body.

The first face she saw was the guide, Brady. He came forward with a smile of relief.

Lea looked around and saw some

large footprints near her current location, and she smiled. "Thank goodness. How long have I been out here?"

He wrapped his arms around her and hugged her. She was shocked at the intimacy, but patted him on his back. "You have been missing for four days. Your phone was alive, but we couldn't get a lock on the signal. There are so many odd nooks and crannies around here."

She nodded. "That must have been it. I don't remember much."

He leaned back. "Really? I would have thought you would have tales of survival to tell."

Lea cleared her throat. "I am not home yet."

He was suddenly all assistance as he helped get her to the nearest search hub. They got the message out that she had been found, and then, she was being brought by snowmobile to an ambulance and from there, a hospital.

Doctor Bethnel came up to her on her second day in hospital. "We have your bloodwork back. We don't know who administered it, but you have some kind of hallucinogen in your system. There are also a few traces of something with a chemical signature similar to rohypnol. You are lucky to be alive."

She was getting dressed and preparing to go home. "Well, it would explain why I don't remember anything and some of the dreams I have been having. Weird shit. Am I free to go?"

He scowled but nodded. "Here. Take this card for a victims' services officer. You were subjected to bruising sexual activity, but we couldn't get any DNA from the source. Whoever he was, he was sterile. We will let you know if any of the disease tests come back positive."

She finished pulling her shirt on. "Right. I will assume everything is fine if

I don't hear back in thirty days."

He frowned. "I don't understand how you were able to survive four days alone, and if you weren't alone, who drugged you. I hate a mystery."

She zipped up her bag. "So do I, but I hate being away from home even more. Once I am in my own territory, I will be able to relax and maybe more memories will come to me. For now, I just want to be home."

She got a cab and headed home. Her car was being towed back to her place. The battery was frozen. It wouldn't start.

Lea was delighted to be home. She went through her fridge and tossed out the expired milk. The rest was salvageable.

She plugged her phone in and walked past the landline with its blinking lights. After coffee and a sandwich, she started playing the messages.

Her mother was worried, her boss

fired her for not turning up on Monday, her boss rehired her, and Brady wanted to know how she was.

She had to admire his tenacity.

With a sense of obligation, she called him and invited him over for coffee. She took a hot shower and tried not to think of huge hands moving on her skin. Lea shivered and got dressed in a long-sleeved tunic, leggings and a wrap.

Her hair was braided over one shoulder when the doorbell rang, and she went to the door to answer it.

Brady smiled slowly. "You are looking well."

She chuckled. "I feel well. Come in. I haven't thanked you yet for finding me."

He had an armload of objects, and he thrust them at her. "These are for you. And it was my job to find you. I lost you."

"It wasn't your fault."

"It was. I should never have taken

Dan's word for it that you were still behind him. He didn't even look." He removed his snowy boots and hung up his coat.

"I went off the trail. Lost control on a corner and skidded to a halt a mile later."

He blinked in surprise. "You remember?"

"All of it, more or less." She shrugged and looked at the objects in her arms. "What is this?"

"Just some small tokens of apology and appreciation. I would also like to take you out to dinner if you haven't eaten already."

She sat and opened the paper holding the bouquet. They weren't roses. Wild snow flowers were in her arms, and they had the sweetest scent. "Where did you find these?"

He shrugged and looked abashed. "I know a spot."

She got the flowers into water, looking at the delicate white blooms and wishing they could stay that way forever. She inhaled deeply, and there was a familiar scent. The water in the hot spring had given everything a distinct odour. These flowers held that undertone.

She was a little bemused when she turned and opened the next parcel. Her fingers went numb when she saw the thick wolf fur.

She looked at him, and he was frowning.

He stroked it. "I had to guess, but this was the one you rubbed your cheek in most often, so I cleaned it up and brought it to you."

Her hands were shaking.

He pressed the final gift into her hands. She opened it numbly, staring at him. Roasted venison was lying in the box.

"See? Now, we don't have to go out

for dinner." He smiled slowly.

"You…"

"Yes?"

She cleared her throat. "I thought your hair was darker."

He grinned. "It is. The human shape is the way we hide in the modern world, but the Sasquatch was the best way to track you. When I found you so near to one of my lairs, it seemed the best place to keep you safe while we waited out the storm."

"The frozen men?"

"Poachers a few decades old. I will eventually put them somewhere to be found. They die in the winter, and I hate for the rot to get them. It makes a mess of my territory."

She shivered, and he moved next to her, putting the joint of meat on the counter. "Why did you… as a beast when we…"

"Ah, the Sasquatch is my natural

form. I learned this one later, as did the doctor who spoke with you at the hospital. It is really difficult to hold this form while mating. I wanted to see if I didn't have to, and I was delighted that you are so responsive."

She was quaking, and her knees collapsed under her. He caught her easily, and with a bit of exploring, he carried her to her bedroom.

She blinked slowly as he set her down in her bed. "Why are you here?"

"I would never leave my mate undefended. I have to say, I enjoy that your home backs onto a national park. I would not have thought it of you, but you did have some good instincts."

He stripped and crawled on top of her. He nuzzled her cheek with his. He kissed her and smiled. "This is easier in this form, but with your scent so heady, I won't be able to hold my shape long."

She blinked. "I just had a shower."

"That isn't what I am smelling." He slid his hand between her thighs. "*This* is what I am scenting. This is the scent that calls to me no matter how distant you are. It was what made it so easy to track you."

She stared at his handsome features, seeing the similarities in the Bigfoot she had taken as her lover. The brow ridge was an echo, the flared nostrils showed similarity in shape, and the lips were the same, though these didn't have fangs behind them.

"You followed the scent of my pussy?"

He waggled his brows. "And your heat. You were ovulating. I had all kinds of incentive to find you and fuck you in a timely manner."

Brady was stroking his hand over her belly with possessive care.

"The doctor said that whatever left traces inside me was sterile."

"He would. He is one of us. You have

met six of us in the last two days, all with different territories and specialities."

He moved his hand under her tunic and stroked her belly. "We will do things in the way of your people. A short courtship, a nice wedding, and then, you will join me in my territory. The baby will look human for a few weeks, and that is when we will register its birth. After that, we can raise it in the woods."

"The woods?"

"I have a nice four thousand-square-foot home that I built for my family. Whenever I started it. I didn't think of having one until you turned up on that tour and then went missing. After that, it has been all I have been focused on."

He pried the waistband of her tights down and slipped his hand between her thighs.

She was so focused on that one thought that she blurted, "I am pregnant?"

He grinned. "Your scent has changed, so I would say yes. We had better consummate this here so that you will have a reasonable explanation."

She was so adrift in her thoughts that she was peeled out of her clothing before she could do more than wriggle around to assist.

He grinned. "I was wondering why you didn't have a bra out there. It seems a common article of clothing."

"My shirt had one built in. It wasn't great, but it kept things in check."

He lifted her and unsnapped her bra. He smiled down at her. "I do love the sight of the marks on you."

Brady leaned over and kissed the pink punctures before he scraped his tongue across her. *That* was familiar. The rough cat-like appendage definitely got her attention. Her nipples hardened, and she felt a rush of moisture between her thighs.

He licked and sucked at her breasts until she squirmed under him. She couldn't think, couldn't focus.

Her breath came faster as he moved down her body until he was scraping his tongue across her clit.

She moaned and mewled, threading her fingers through his hair as she parted her thighs and bent her knees so that she was braced on the bed. She felt him smile against her skin, and he drove a few fingers into her wet cream, sliding them easily into her.

He took her body's response as an invitation and surged upward, covering her and driving into her in one long thrust.

She dimly heard a sound. Her front door was opening.

Brady smiled and kissed her, thrusting slowly and rhythmically as footfalls got closer.

The sight of her fleeing back preceded the gasp and view of the friend who had roped her into the ski trip.

The sound of the door slamming was something that finally broke Brady's kiss. "Do you think she saw enough?"

Lea frowned. "You did that on purpose."

He pulled back and grinned. "Better her see that than this."

She groaned as he expanded, his body growing two feet in seconds, and the fur that touched her inner thighs added an extra stimulation to the increasing pressure of the widening cock inside her.

He thrust carefully into her, and she stared up at the now-familiar face. "This is going to take some getting used to."

He grinned, showing a lot of fang. "Take your time, dearest. I am not going anywhere."

He thrust deep and gritted his teeth as his cock jerked into her.

Son of a bitch. He can talk. And when she realized that, that was the part that most distressed her... she knew she had lost her mind.

Camping Out

Sara, bridesmaid extraordinaire, was tired of weddings. If she had to watch one more dopey bride marry one more clueless groom, she was going to scream.

Now, she was the victim of a team exercise. She was on a camping trip with the other members of the Brad and Jessica bridal party, but she was the only one solo. The others had all been couples chosen to reinforce the love of the bride and groom. She had been chosen because she could make a wedding run, and Jessica didn't want to hire an organizer.

Sara just had to remain here until

dawn. Then, the camping was over and she could claim work obligations to pull her back to the normal world.

The others left the fire for the semi-privacy of their tents, and Sara was treated to the sounds of four couples having sex in the outdoors.

She looked around the nylon walls of her tent, lifted the edge of the t-shirt she was sleeping in and slid one hand into her panties. She had always been a join-er.

Sara thought that she was being qui-et, but after a few minutes, she heard a scratching at the fly of her tent. She had pitched her tent a solid distance from the others for exactly that reason.

Unable to continue her activities with someone scratching at her tent, she pulled her fingers out of her underwear, tugged down her shirt and opened the top zipper of the tent in case it was something small and fuzzy that wanted entrance.

A vine lashed around her mouth and nose, additional vines wrapped around her torso, and she was pulled out of the tent without being able to whisper a word.

Her lungs ached, and she wanted to scream, but she needed to breathe more. She was hauled across the forest floor; bits of bracken struck her and jabbed at her skin. Her arms were tied to her sides, and she was pulled along with the scent of sap in her nostrils and only tantalizing gasps of air that made it through.

Sara didn't know how long she had been pulled through the woods, but when the vines hauled her onto a wide wooden platform, she was sore, damaged and relieved. She was strapped down on her back with her gaze to the sky.

The vines remained over her mouth

and others bound her arms and legs down.

"What have you brought me?" The voice resonated through the clearing.

The leaves on the vines rustled a low whisper.

Laughter rippled through the woods with that same low, resonant voice. "She was seeking pleasure in my woods? There was no male with her?"

The rustles answered him.

"Prove it."

To her humiliation, the vines jacked her right hand into the air.

She heard the approach of the male speaker. When he arrived next to her, she tried to flinch away, but there was nowhere to go. Either she was looking at a naked, well-endowed man with the head of a stag, or she was a lunatic.

The man bent and sniffed at her imprisoned hand, lapping out with his tongue. He laughed. "So she was. Well spotted. Now, little human, what do you desire?"

He walked over to her head, and he bent down, looking her in the eye.

She felt him crawling through her mind, seeking out her fantasies and sensitivities. She was humiliated at some of the thoughts he turned over, but he continued on.

When he finished the touch on her mind, he stood straight, and the deer's head changed to a boar, bear, lion, rabbit and stranger animals than she could imagine. Finally, he settled with a human face with smaller antlers on either side of his skull.

His hair was long and a dark red; his face had been pulled from her fantasies.

The wide brown eyes were the only portion of him that still resembled the stag, aside from the horns.

Fear was flipping her stomach, but her instincts were on alert for any sign of reciprocated interest.

He smiled at her. "I think you would be more comfortable if we made a few changes."

She thought he meant to untie her, but instead, a vine snaked under the neckline of her shirt and split it in two. Another vine did the same with her panties. One moment she was semi-clothed, the next, the vines and branches were pulling the fabric away from her.

She shivered and held her breath, waiting for what happened next.

"Well, we will begin by warming your interest."

He walked slowly around her, trailing his fingers over her breasts, belly and the tops of her thighs. He circled slowly, over and over. Each time, his fingers took a different path, and she tried to twist to put his touch where she wanted it.

The moon was rising overhead, and

he followed her gaze. "Yes, lovely, isn't it? Once a year, I come out here, to these woods, and I ask the moon for a companion. This year, the woods answered me. I do apologize that it might not have been what you wanted, but I am in dire straits."

She frowned. She was the one tied to the damned wood, and he was in dire straits?

He chuckled. "Once a year, I have a chance to ask. You have not wondered how many times there was no response. It was more times than your cities have been in this area. There used to be sacrifices, you know. A maiden offered to me, and after I had her, she was given to a warrior of high standing as a reward for him. His woman had been honoured, and I would always watch over my lovers."

She squirmed. She was no maiden.

He laughed. "I know you are no

maiden. It will be easier for you. One night of sacrifice for lifelong honour."

She narrowed her eyes at him and wondered what kind of honour.

"Health, happiness, and if you wished for another visit, I would be happy to oblige."

She had no idea how you could make someone happy, but she was facing her ideal lover, and it would be foolish to waste the opportunity.

He grinned and trailed his fingers over her breasts. "While I will try and cater to your desires, I have a few of my own, and your breasts are lovely."

He stood at her left side and sucked at her left breast with hot ferocity. He leaned over and did the same to the right, moving between them as she squirmed slightly on the wood.

It wasn't fair that biology created an instant attachment between human women and anything suckling at their breasts. Her lids lowered and her fear faded, and it had nothing to do with her.

He caressed her mounds of flesh with his hands and stroked the nipples with his thumbs when he wasn't sucking them.

She felt her clit throb a little with the sucking and tugging. Her position was ridiculous by any standard. When she woke up, she was going to have to stop eating wedding cake. That stuff would give you nightmares.

Her would-be lover moved to stand near her feet, and he crawled up and onto the altar, over her. He continued his gentle mauling of her breasts, and she was a little surprised when something started sliding between her folds.

He had complete focus on her reddening mounds while something slid between her lower lips and delved into her. She jerked, and another something or other squirted something on her ass and slid inside.

There was a slight burning as whatever stickiness it used shocked her skin, but it was more her senses, because whatever it was had been cold.

The two thin invaders moved softly inside her, and she fought the escalating sensations that wanted to be released with a slow circuit of her clit.

The beast-man moved down her body, and with what appeared to be a silent command, had the vines lift her off the wooden altar.

He chuckled at the vine invasion she was undergoing. "I can manage."

The vines inside her retreated, but she had a dark suspicion that she wanted the one in her ass back again. She quickly blanked that train of thought, but it had been there.

The vine came back and slid into her ass again.

Her lover was watching the entire

thing, and when the vine was slowly moving in and out of her ass again, he leaned in and sucked her clit between his teeth.

She would have moaned, but she was gagged. He lapped at her with the slow stroke of a tongue that changed texture with every swipe.

The violent shivering of her orgasm struck without warning. She bucked against his mouth and felt his grin. It was the same smirk that all men gave when they licked their partner to climax.

He moved over her and pressed into her; the odd thing was that his penis changed shape with every thrust. She held her breath, not knowing what the next one was going to feel like. This was not in her fantasies. She had never imagined anything like this before.

She moaned behind her green gag. The vine in her ass doubled in size somehow and thrust rapidly. It was double timing his thrusts.

She felt the building of tension once again and watched the moon as it appeared and disappeared over his shoulder as he thrust. Her body tensed around him, and she squeezed down hard. He thrust deep, and she bucked against him as her body lost control.

The anal invader removed itself, and she sighed a moment before her lover jerked into her hard and shook with his own release. Short, sharp jabs with his hips kept him inside her as his body reached its own conclusion.

Sara lay back, and he draped himself over her. The restraints slithered away, including her gag.

She sucked in air as fast as she could. She shivered. "Can I go now?"

It was apparently the wrong thing to say.

He lifted his head and stared at her. "You can go free if you can outrun me."

She looked at him in shock. "What?"

"You heard me. Every time you run and I catch you, I will fuck you, one way or another. I read your mind, you like games. If you want to be free of me, make it back to your campsite before I catch you. Then, you can go."

She squirmed. He was still hard inside her. "I didn't mean..."

"Yes, you did." He levered up and off her.

He extended his hand and helped her to her feet. He slapped her on the ass. "Now, run."

Naked and barefoot, she sprinted for the treeline. Her legs didn't want to work together, but she got them stepping in time as she headed for the largest clump of trees she could see. The moon wasn't any help here. Light wouldn't come until morning.

She stumbled, holding the trees and touching the bark for support. She could smell sweat, and it had only been a few minutes. Cum was trailing down her thighs, and a blind man could have found her in the dark. Her hunter was far from blind.

She rounded a tree and ran straight into him. She shrieked and he grinned.

"It seems I have caught you. Kneel."

She sighed in relief. This was going to be easy.

She knelt, and when he pressed his cock to her lips, she took him inside, tasting the musk that she had left behind as well as his own wild scent. He throbbed in her mouth as she sucked on the instroke and again on the backstroke. She couldn't take him all, no matter what she wanted.

She cupped his balls and rolled them gently as she sucked him. When she felt the sack tighten, she pulled away and leaned sharply, letting the cum splatter over her shoulder and against the tree.

He groaned low, and when the small jets had ceased, he looked down at her. "Run."

She got to her feet and ran, making her way as quickly as she could. Her eyes were getting used to the darkness, and it was easier to move through the trees. They seemed to move aside to make pathways for her, and she got much further before he dropped out of a tree and pinned her against it.

He lifted her and wrapped her hands around a branch above her head. "Hold tight."

He pressed her against the tree, bracing her weight with his hips before he moved his cock between her thighs and pushing into her. He cupped her thighs and pulled her away from the tree, which had the effect of bending her back as her arms still held on. Her legs wrapped tightly around his waist, and he started to pump into her.

Her breasts jiggled. He sucked one into his mouth and then the next. Her backbend position made it impossible for her to catch her balance. He cupped her buttocks and pounded upward, stretching her and delving deep. She screamed loud and long when her orgasm struck, and he let out a deep howl when he jerked and jetted into her over and over.

There had to be a fertility element to him, because no regular male could repeatedly produce that much cum.

When he leaned her back on the tree, he eased her legs down and stroked her arms to get her to release them.

She placed her hands on his chest for a moment before lowering them.

His whisper in her ear was almost enough to make her cry. "Run."

She moved around him and tried to get her exhausted limbs to cooperate. She shifted and hid as well as she could.

Through the trees, she could see the embers from the campfire. She was nearly back.

Hands grabbed her and pulled her back against a firm body. "Ah ah ah. Got you."

He bent her over a deadfall and was inside her before she could say anything. He used his cum on his fingers and slid one and then another into her ass as he fucked her hard.

She rocked back and forth on the log, trying to brace herself, to push back. He shoved her forward, and she scrabbled on the bark, trying to brace herself as the girth of him slid through her swollen channel.

The aching burn of her ass brought her over the edge with a few of the jolting thrusts. When she was recovering, he pulled out of her and thrust into her ass, sliding deep and using her ass as hard as he had fucked her pussy just moments earlier.

She sobbed as her senses were over-loaded, and when he groaned and slumped against her, she was throbbing with pain and missed satisfaction.

He pulled out of her and whispered again, "Run."

She tried to get up, but her body wouldn't cooperate. "I can't."

He stroked her hair. "Good. Go back to your people and expect to gain your reward."

She slowly turned to face him. "I don't want a reward."

He kissed her softly. "You will have one."

She left him with surprising reluctance and headed for the light of the fire. She crept out of the woods and made a run for her tent with bruised breasts and cum soaking her thighs. She was a mess.

When she arrived at her tent, she looked back, and the moon was setting in time to see dawn begin. The silhouette of the stag-headed man was standing at the edge of the forest, and while she looked, he turned away and returned to his domain.

She blinked and crawled into her tent, wiping herself down and getting dressed. She packed up and got out of there. She just wanted to wake up in her own bed with it all being a dream, but the teeth marks on her breasts were going to make that a little tricky.

She hauled her stuff to her car and got on the road. Reward, huh? She would see.

One month later, Sara was at her desk when her manager arrived in the doorway.

"Sara, can you come with me please? Our new boss has just arrived."

The company had been bought out by a conglomerate known for tearing down the little businesses and cherry picking the employees who would be allowed to continue on the new path.

The boss had his back to her, but his wide shoulders and narrow waist were obvious even through his suit. The dark-red ponytail was a little non-standard, but if he had the money to buy the company, he could do what he wanted with his coiffure.

"Have a seat. Terrance, you may go."

When they door to the executive office closed, he turned slowly. "Sara, is it?"

She had to close her mouth with a snap. This man was the spitting image of her fantasy man from the forest. "Yes. Yes, it is."

He sat across from her. "My name is Oberon Hart. I have just purchased this business, and everyone who works for it, works for me. That includes you."

She nodded. "I am aware of it."

He smiled, and her heart flipped at that smile. "I have looked through your file, and aside from an astonishing amount of time off booked for weddings, you are a model employee. What would you say to Terrence's position?"

She frowned. "Where would he be?"

"Not your concern." He folded his long fingers on the table.

"I am not going to take someone else's position, so if you are going to fire him, fire me first and get it over with." She crossed her arms over her chest and scowled at him.

He looked her over for a moment before he nodded. "Good. I believe I have just found my new assistant."

That turn around was fast. "What?"

"I am in need of a new assistant, and I would like one that cannot be bribed or bullied." He twisted his lips in a calculated smirk. "Are you interested?"

She stared at him and asked blankly.

"What is the salary and are there bene-fits?"

He gave her a number triple her an-nual salary. "You are staring at me, Sara. Is there a reason for it?"

She shook her head slowly. "No. You just remind me of someone I thought I met a while ago."

He quirked his lips. "I have one of those faces. So, you accept?"

She nodded. "Yes. When do I start?"

"The desk outside this office is yours. When you move your stuff over, the new pay hike commences."

She got to her feet, and he rose to his. He came around his desk and shook her hand. She felt a strange vibration at the contact.

He turned her toward the door, and as she exited, he whispered, "Run, Sara. Run."

She whirled, but the door closed.

Oberon Hart was a tough but fair boss. Aside from that one reference, she was now doubting that the man in the office behind her was the one she was thinking of. The man she couldn't stop thinking of.

She kept the same hours that he did, so it was inevitable that she would eventually be there late in the evening after everyone had gone home.

She prepared the payroll assessment that broke down everyone's rates and their productivity and headed into his office with a brusque knock.

He looked up from his documents and smiled. "What is it, Sara?"

"I have the report, and it is nearing nine o'clock. If you aren't going to pack it in, I will pitch a tent at my desk."

He took his paperwork from her. "Is it that cute little nylon tent again? I have to admit that the sight of you jumping into it like it would keep me from following was the height of amusing."

She felt her legs wobble. "Who told you about that?"

"About the tent, or you covered with cum sprinting through the woods, leaving a scent trail a mile wide? Even when the trees helped you, they couldn't hide you. You reeked of sex."

She blushed and stumbled back. Every woman's nightmare. Being reminded of what she had done the night before.

Sara faced him and looked around. "What are you doing here?"

"Oh, I have a life in the human world. I am just forced into my natural form once a year. Usually alone in those woods. I think that I will enjoy your company next year. The horns didn't faze you for more than a minute."

He got up and came around the desk. "I promised you a reward, but it has been hard to arrange, so I thought that I would offer you companionship and reward you via that route."

She blinked. "Companionship?"

He took her by the hips and plonked her on the edge of his desk. He slid his hands up under her skirt and peeled her panties and pantyhose down past her knees. It restricted her range of movement and made her nervous about what was coming next.

He reached between her thighs and eased two fingers into her. Just talking to him had made her wet, and he was discovering it.

He smiled slowly. "Yes. Companionship. Modern clothing has a lot of layers, but I believe I can work around it."

He opened his trousers and stepped between her thighs.

She said in husky tones, "There are sexual harassment laws in place."

"I am not harassing you; I have made an offer, and you have accepted it. We are just sealing the deal."

He fit his cock to her, and he eased into her while she leaned back on her hands. When he was fully seated, he whispered, "Open your blouse."

She awkwardly leaned to one side and unbuttoned her blouse with her free hand. When she had her blouse open, he eyed her breasts.

"Bring them out for me."

She improvised by unsnapping her bra at the back and lifting the cups free of her flesh.

He bent forward, suckling hard at one and then the other.

He was hard and hot inside her, and as he sucked, he slowly moved. The pleasure built, and she threaded a hand through his crimson locks. She held his head to her breasts as he rocked into her.

He grazed her skin with his teeth and pounded forward with short jerks of his hips.

The jolts pushed her over the edge, and she clutched at his shoulder while she opened her mouth in a silent scream.

Fire burned along every nerve, and it continued while he stroked inside her and out again in a frenzied motion. As he came, he groaned against her breasts.

The air between them smelled of sex. She took in the surroundings of the office and just realized that she had become the world's biggest cliché.

He lifted his head and looked at her. "You are not happy?"

"I just fucked my boss on his desk. Sex at the office isn't appropriate."

He wrinkled his nose. "I can work from home if you would prefer to fuck me there. As long as you fuck me, I don't care."

"Until I get old and wrinkly and you find another woman."

"You will remain as you are. The

moon decreed it. You are not immortal, but you are ageless." He nipped at her neck.

"If you work from home, you won't need me."

His grip on her tightened. "I need you. You are my first self-sacrifice that didn't weep when I took her. If I had known how much fun it would be, I would have insisted that the girls not be maidens." He winked.

She rolled her eyes. He was still inside her and still as hard as ever. "We can't continue this here. I have to face these people and the cleaners will talk about cum on all the surfaces."

He nodded as if deciding. "From my home then. I will show you where it is."

She blinked slowly. "Now?"

"I do some of my best work in the moonlight. Come on." He slid out of her and tucked his cock in his tailored trousers. There was a cum stain around his fly, but he didn't seem to mind.

She got up and slid her panties into place. Her pantyhose were just going to get in the way. She kicked off her shoes, peeled off the nylon and wadded it in a ball. With her shoes back on and her skirt down, she only had to try and wrestle her bra into place before doing up her blouse.

She grabbed her purse on the way out, and he escorted her to his vehicle, driving with tremendous skill for someone who kept one hand on her inner thigh. It was very distracting.

The house that he drove them to was on a wilderness property. The rustic cabin was at odds with his sports car and polished exterior.

He came around the car and lifted her against his chest, carrying her into the house. He seemed to relax the moment she was over the threshold.

His kiss was sudden, but the intensity

couldn't be ignored. He definitely wanted her, and that was the best aphrodisiac
there was.

She moaned as he pulled her blouse
out of the skirt where she had tucked it.
He walked with her into the kitchen and
bent her over the counter; she inhaled
sharply when his tugging freed her shirt
and her belly and then breasts touched
the icy granite.

He pulled her bra off and tossed it to
the floor before he unzipped her skirt.
When it hit the floor, she was wearing
her panties and her heels. Her panties
met their end next.

They were still around her ankles,
and it kept her legs together when he
thrust into her again from the rear.

He reached under her, and his arms
cupped her breasts, kneading and
squeezing as he moved inside her.

She grabbed the countertop and held
on as he thrust into her while he held

her breasts in an arousing grip.

When she started to shake, he increased his pace and she let out a gasping moan while he bellowed into the empty kitchen.

He pulled out of her and kissed his way down her spine. "I have someone here who wants to say hello."

He lifted her again and carried her to his greenhouse or arboretum. "You made an impression on them, and they wanted to repay you. Ours will be an odd union, but I couldn't have found you without them."

He set her on a wooden slab, and vines lovingly came around her limbs, lifting her in the air before she was penetrated anally and vaginally with the vines twisting inside her.

The coils wrapping around her breasts were in a frenzy of excitement, and Sara opened her mouth to call to Oberon for help. The gag slid across her mouth, leaving her holding a sapling between her teeth.

She never agreed to the threesome with a forest.

About the Author

A fusion of two author names, Viola Masters enjoys frolicking in the dark parts of societal norms where political correctness dares not tread. (Or just goofing around in the grim stuff, take your pick.)

Her stories are a start for your own fantasies to twist the tale to your own purposes. There is a Viola Masters Facebook group if you want to share what you would like to see in further installments.

www.ingramcontent.com/pod-product-compliance
Lightning Source LLC
Chambersburg PA
CBHW071932190726
48293CB00004B/1243